THUMBELINA

Illustrated by Melinda J Stirk
Story re-told by Kenneth Keay

Published by Anker International Plc.,

Code SBD

A TALE FROM THE LAND OF NOD...™

Once upon a time there was an old woman who longed for a child. In the early Spring she went to see a good witch who sold her a single seed.

"Plant this seed," the witch told her, "and tend it carefully as it grows."

The old lady did as she was told and a few days later a seedling appeared, which became a single stalk on which a flower bud appeared.

One morning the old lady went to the flower and saw that it was open. Curled up in it fast asleep was a tiny girl, no taller than half the length of the old lady's thumb.

"Oh, what a beautiful child," murmured the old woman to herself, "she is so tiny that I will call her Thumbelina."

The old woman found half a walnut shell, which she cleaned and polished to make a bed for Thumbelina. In the bottom she put violet petals for a mattress and found a sweet-smelling rose petal for a coverlet. Then she took a fine silk handkerchief and made dresses for the little girl. Gently the old woman blew onto the flower. Thumbelina awoke, and was so thrilled to have such beautiful clothes and such a comfortable bed, that she sang the most beautiful song the old woman had ever heard. The sound filled the whole house. Thumbelina and the old lady were very happy together.

One Summer day as Thumbelina was singing, an old toad was hopping by, and stopped to listen to her lovely song. He hopped over to the window, looked in and there saw Thumbelina sitting in her walnut shell bed.

"She will make a good wife for my son," he croaked, and that night the old toad crept into the cottage, picked up Thumbelina's bed, in which she was still asleep and carried her off, He put the bed on a water lily leaf, and swam off to find his son.

"I have found you a bride," said the old toad. "Make haste and build a home for her between the reeds in the swamp."

The toad's son went off to start building, and the old one went back to Thumbelina.

He jumped onto the leaf and woke her up.

"You are to be my son's bride," he said, "now give me your bed so that he can put it in the house he is building for you." Thumbelina jumped out of bed onto the leaf as the old toad picked up the walnut shell in his mouth and swam away.

As dawn broke, Thumbelina, sitting alone on her leaf, began to cry. Suddenly a fish popped his head out of the water and said, "Why are you crying, pretty maid? What can be wrong?" Thumbelina told him all about the toad's son.

"Well", said the fish, "I can soon help you. I'll just nibble through the stalk of the leaf and you can float free!"

With that he dived under the water, and a few minutes later, Thumbelina felt her leaf drifting gently down the stream. The fish popped his head out of the water and called, "Good-bye, good luck."

The old toad came back just as Thumbelina sailed round a bend in the stream.

"Come back, come back," he shouted, "you are going to marry my son, he's just building you a house!" But Thumbelina did not hear him.

She floated down the stream on her leaf, past trees and fields and the houses of a small town until she drifted into a broad river that flowed very slowly through open countryside.

After a while a beautiful butterfly fluttered down "Where are you off to?" she asked Thumbelina "Will you be my friend?"

"Of course," said Thumbelina. "Come sit with me on my leaf."

So they sat together while Thumbelina told her story, and after a while the butterfly said "If you tie your sash around my waist I can pull you along faster."

So Thumbelina took her sash and wound it around the butterfly's tiny waist, and very soon she was floating past more trees and fields as she was pulled along.

After a while the butterfly called "I can't pull you any more, for I am tired now and must rest." She pulled the leaf to the bank and Thumbelina untied her sash. "Thank you," she said as the butterfly flew away, "Oh! thank you."

"Good-bye," the butterfly called, "good luck." Thumbelina was all alone as she made her way through the tall grass, until she found a flat space that would make a good home, beneath a broad oak tree in the forest.

She found short grass stalks to thatch a roof over a gap between two roots, a piece of soft moss to use as a bed, and for blankets she wove a quilt of thistledown.

As Summer wore on Thumbelina became friends with many of the insects, birds and animals that lived in the wood, and they would often gather and listen as she sang her sweet songs.

Summer turned to Autumn and as Winter came closer many of her friends hid away or curled up for a long sleep until Spring came once more. The first frosts came, and poor Thumbelina began to search further and further away for a warmer place to live. One day, she became hopelessly lost, and as night fell and frost began to creep in, she curled up shivering, under a leaf and began to cry.

She was very surprised when she heard a voice say "Who is that, why are you crying?"

Peeping out from under the leaf she saw before her a plump little fieldmouse dressed in a blue dress with a bright yellow apron.

"My name is Thumbelina," she sobbed, "I'm searching for a new house where I can live for the winter and now I'm lost."

"There, there, don't cry," said the fieldmouse, "I'm Felicity Fieldmouse and I've plenty of space in my house. It's nice and warm there and I have plenty of food. You could come and live with me and keep me company through the long winter."

Thumbelina stopped sobbing, "I would love to," she said, "and I can sew and weave."

"Then we have a bargain," said Felicity, "let's go home."

The field mouse led Thumbelina to a bright green door set in a bank beneath a hedge, and into a cosy little room where a cheerful fire burned in the hearth.

"I'm sure you will be comfortable here" said the fieldmouse.

"Oh, I will be" said Thumbelina as she fell asleep in a comfortable chair beside the fire.

Winter came and the first snow, but Thumbelina was warm and snug in the little house. One day Felicity said, "We are to have a visitor tonight, it's Mr Mole, a very fine gentleman. He has heard all about you and would like to meet you."

"I've never ever seen Mr Mole," said Thumbelina.

"Ah," said Felicity, "that is because Mr Mole does not like daylight, but he has a very large home and tunnels all over the place."

Mr Mole arrived later that evening. He was quite stout, with a beautiful shiny black coat. He wore little gold spectacles on the tip of his nose and was very polite.

As he was about to leave he said to Thumbelina "You must come to visit me. I will call tomorrow and fetch you," he said as he shuffled away.

Felicity was very excited, "Mr Mole must like you a lot," she said, "he doesn't often ask anyone to his home."

The next day Mr Mole led the two friends into one of the many tunnels which led to his house. After a while they came upon a hole in the tunnel roof and beneath it a swallow, lying very still.

"The silly bird should have gone far away before the cold weather arrived," the mole said, "but I suppose he crawled in here and died. I will clear him out when I have more time in the Spring."

Felicity and Mr Mole hurried on down the tunnel, but Thumbelina stood looking at the beautiful bird. She placed her hand on the bird's breast and felt a tiny tremble.

"Oh, you are still alive" she cried excitedly. "I'll be back" said Thumbelina, "I'll be back soon," and went to catch up with Felicity and Mr Mole.

Although Mr Mole's house was warm and very clean Thumbelina thought it was very dark and gloomy, and when she asked him why there were no windows he replied, "I don't like the daylight, it hurts my eyes."

The two friends returned home, and Felicity was very excited. "Mr Mole is looking for a wife," she chattered, "and he asked me if I thought that you would marry him. I said that perhaps you would. He is a fine gentleman." Thumbelina said nothing, but she knew she could not live in dark tunnels for the rest of her life.

After Felicity had gone to bed, Thumbelina crept into the tunnel to where the swallow lay, taking with her water and a blanket from her bed.

She poured a little of the water into the bird's beak, and put the blanket over him.

"I'll be back tomorrow," she said and saw one of the swallow's eyelids flicker a little.

Each day Thumbelina went to the swallow taking him food and water, and each day he grew stronger, until in the early Spring he was strong enough to squeeze out of the tunnel and fly away. Before he went he said to Thumbelina "Watch out for me, and if you ever need me, stand near this hole and call. I will hear you!"

Summer came back once more and Thumbelina spent as much time as she could in the sunshine, collecting the bright flowers that made Felicity's house look cheerful.

Mr Mole made more and more trips to visit Thumbelina, but always after the bright daylight

had gone. One day he came in with a small box in his hand.

He knelt before Thumbelina and said "My dear Thumbelina, will you marry me?"

Before poor Thumbelina could open her mouth, Felicity said "Of course she will, won't you dear," and then went on, "and we'll have an Autumn wedding and invite just everybody!"

Poor Thumbelina. She didn't really want to marry Mr Mole and spend all her life in dark tunnels below the ground, but Felicity had been so kind to her that she didn't want to upset her.

As the wedding day came nearer, Thumbelina spent as much time in the bright sunlight amongst the flowers as she could. Felicity didn't seem to notice as she spent every day happily sewing and making Thumbelina's wedding dress.

On the day before the wedding, Thumbelina was sitting in the sunshine looking very sad when suddenly she heard a whistle, and her friend the swallow landed on the ground before her.

"Why are you so sad," he asked, "on a day so bright and beautiful as this?"

Thumbelina told him that next day she was to marry Mr Mole, and after her wedding she would never again see the sun and the flowers.

The swallow looked at her and said softly, "Why not come with me, for I am about to leave and fly south to a much warmer country. Quickly now climb upon my back and we'll be on our way!"

"Oh thank you, thank you," cried Thumbelina doing as she was bid.

"I shall miss Felicity but I could never live in Mr Mole's cold, damp tunnels, and see no sunshine or flowers."

The swallow flew high into the sky and turned southwards. When it became cold during the night, Thumbelina snuggled into his feathers, but during the day she lay in the sunshine holding lightly to his neck. Below them as they flew even further south, the countryside changed from green grass and trees to bright rocks and sand, until at last, in a land far away, the swallow flew into a garden in which hundreds of bright flowers grew, and sat quietly as Thumbelina climbed into one of the sweet smelling blooms.

She had scarcely stepped down when she heard the soft tinkle of laughter. She stood up and peered out of the flower, and had the happiest surprise of her life for, from almost every flower around her, a bright smiling face looked out.

"Welcome, welcome," they all cried, and Thumbelina realised that at last she was amongst her own people, the Flower Fairies.

"Come and join us," they shouted, and to Thumbelina's surprise each fairy opened a pair of crystal clear wings and flew down to the ground.

"But I don't have any wings," she called and was about to climb down the flower stem, when a soft voice said, "What is your name, for you are certainly the most beautiful of all my people?"

Thumbelina turned and standing before her was the most handsome man she had ever seen, the King of the Fairies.

"My name, your Majesty, is Thumbelina," she said, curtseying to the King.

"That is no name for someone so beautiful as you," replied the King. "I shall call you Maia, for that means 'most beautiful of all',"
He gave her a pair of gossamer wings.
"Put these on," he said, "and join us."
Thumbelina flew down with the King to where all the other Fairies were gathered.